For Johanna and Danny
—P.C.

With love to Frank and Joan
—C.W.

Library of Congress Cataloging-in-Publication Data
Cooper, Patrick.   Never trust a squirrel/ by Patrick Cooper; illustrated by Catherine Walters.—1st American ed.   p. cm.
Summary: When William the guinea pig finds himself in a life-threatening situation
while exploring with a squirrel, he learns an important lesson about trust.
ISBN 0-525-46009-8 (hardcover) [1. Trust (Psychology)—Fiction. 2. Guinea pigs—Fiction. 3. Squirrels—Fiction.]
I. Walters, Catherine, date ill. II. Title. PZ7.C78765Ng 1999[E]—dc21 98-23251 CIP AC

Published in the United States 1999 by Dutton Children's Books,
a division of Penguin Putnam Books for Young Readers · 345 Hudson Street, New York, New York 10014
http://www.penguinputnam.com/yreaders/index.htm

Originally published in Great Britain 1998 by Magi Publications, London
Typography by Alan Carr · Printed in Belgium · First American Edition
2 4 6 8 10 9 7 5 3 1

Never Trust a SQUIRREL!

PATRICK COOPER

illustrated by CATHERINE WALTERS

DUTTON CHILDREN'S BOOKS
New York

It was a beautiful day, and William the guinea pig was bored. He sat staring out of his hutch, wondering what to do next.

He thought about asking his mother for ideas, but he knew what she would say: "Play a game of hide-the-pellet" or "Chew on some hay." His mother could always find things to do, but they were dull, guinea-pig things.

William sighed. He was just about to close his eyes for a nap when, suddenly, a squirrel dropped out of the nut tree and looked in at him.

"Hiya," said the squirrel. "I'm Stella. Who are you?"

"William," said William hopefully. Maybe Stella would invite him to play. Squirrels seemed to have a lot of fun chasing one another around the yard and chattering in the trees.

Sure enough, Stella said, "Well, William, I'm going exploring. Want to come?"

But before he could answer, she scampered back up the branch and across the treetops.

"Wait," said William, but she was gone. And he couldn't run into the yard to look for her, because he wasn't allowed out of the hutch without his mother.

Being a guinea pig was hard, but being a young guinea pig was worse.

William watched for Stella until bedtime, but there was no sign of his new friend.

That night his mother promised, "We'll go for a long walk tomorrow, William. You'll like that."

But William had other plans. . . .

The next day, Stella appeared at their door.

"Come into the woods and play," she chittered.

"I can't get out," said William sadly. "The door is locked."

"I'll fix that," said Stella, and she nibbled off the catch.

"William," cried his mother, "stay here. The woods aren't safe for guinea pigs."

But William didn't listen.

The two adventurers reached the cool shade of
the trees.

"Let's climb!" Stella suggested. She scampered up
a tree trunk.

"Okay," said William eagerly. He made a running
start, grabbed at the bark with his tiny paws, and
rolled back into the grass. Guinea pigs can't climb.

"Silly old guinea pig," said Stella, laughing.

"I can play hide-and-seek," offered William.

William hid in a piece
of old drainpipe. He
stayed very still, and
Stella couldn't find him.

"I give up!" said Stella crossly. She liked to win every game. "This is stupid. Let's play chase instead."

William chased Stella down the hill. He was
having so much fun that he didn't hear the blackbird at first.

"Run! Run!" it squawked. "Fox! Run, run!"
William was terrified.

"Wh-what do we do now?" he stammered.

"Easy," said Stella. "We just run up a tree."

"But I can't climb!" wailed William.

"Oh, right," said Stella. "That's too bad. Well,
I'll see you later."

And the squirrel was gone again.

"Fox! fox!" called the blackbird.
"Hide, guinea pig, hide!"

But where? William looked around
wildly, then dived under some low
branches and fallen leaves.

He stayed very still, hoping the fox
was no better at searching than Stella.

The leaves quivered. William saw a black nose and sharp, pointed teeth. He felt the fox's warm breath as it rooted through the leaves.

William buried himself deeper, but the movement alerted the fox. It gave a yelp of excitement and scrabbled at the leaf pile.

THUD!

The fox jumped back as the drainpipe came thumping down the hill. Behind it came William's mother. The pipe rolled to a stop near William. "Quick!" called his mother. "Get in!" The frightened guinea pig darted into one end of the pipe. His mother rushed into the other.

She held him close as the fox poked its nose into the pipe. It tried one end, then it tried the other end. It shook the pipe and rolled it, trying to dislodge the little guinea pigs. But William and his mother stayed deep inside, huddled together.

And then the fox gave up. William and his
mother waited inside the pipe just to be sure.

At last the blackbird sang, "All clear! The fox is gone." William's mother peeked out of the pipe and said, "It's time to go home, little one."

William raced back to the hutch and hid in the straw. He was sure his mother was angry with him.

But when she spoke, her voice was soft. "William, I'll take you exploring tomorrow. And if you learn to be careful, someday you can go alone. But you must listen to me from now on.

"And William," she added, "never trust a squirrel."

"Okay," William squeaked.

And he didn't.